LINDA MURDOCK

RAINBOW
of hope

AN INSIDER'S PERSPECTIVE ON AIDS

FOCUS
PUBLISHING, INC.
1375 Washington Avenue South
Bemidji, Minnesota 56601

Rainbow of Hope
An Insider's Perspective on AIDS
by Linda Murdock

First Printing
January, 1996

*All scripture references are from the New International
Version of the Bible.*

Cover Design by Robert A. Yuretich

ISBN 1-885904-07-X

PRINTED IN THE UNITED STATES OF AMERICA
BY
FOCUS PUBLISHING, INC.
1375 Washington Avenue South
Bemidji, Minnesota 56601

This book is dedicated

to

The Glory of God

Foreword

I have had the privilege of knowing Linda Murdock for about seven years. She came to us through the invitation of a woman who saw in Linda, "A diamond in the rough." Our church family was compassionate but uninformed about AIDS. After a medical doctor presented a seminar on AIDS at our church, we were ready to reach out. Linda began faithfully attending and serving our church at that time. The doors of opportunity have opened for Linda to speak in numerous places. Her message includes vital information about HIV, and most important, her testimony about her salvation experience through Jesus Christ. She has been used of the Lord to give hope to those who have none. She has seen the restoration of her own family including the recent contact with her two daughters.

Linda's life story takes you to the edge of hopelessness, then comforts you by showing the mercy and grace of God at work. I believe that God has extended her life that she may continue telling about the wonderful grace of Jesus. When God sees fit to take her home, she will fully realize the meaning of her ministry which is on her business card, "Love Is Never Dying Alone."

Pastor "Chip" Thompson
New England Bible Church
Andover, Massachusetts

Contents

Chapter 1
A Stormy Beginning

I sat in the courtroom feeling nauseated, not knowing whether it was from the heroin, cocaine, or just nerves. It seemed that my name was going to be the last one called. I knew it wouldn't be good news one way or the other, so I sat back and enjoyed my high, not caring how long it would take.

This wasn't the first time that I had been in this courtroom on various charges. The charges were prostitution, possession of drugs, and possession of a hypodermic syringe, but that was enough. The same judge had seen my face once too often and I didn't really expect to walk out of the courtroom free and easy as I had before. Still, there was something about this room; something somber and sobering. Surrounded by dark wood paneling and leather seats, I was aware of hushed voices. I watched the clerk sitting properly at her machine, her face expressionless. A uniformed policeman stood at attention like a wooden soldier. Sliding down into my seat, I looked around. Where was that judge anyway? My eyes focused on the only colorful thing in the front of the room, the American flag. I was suddenly overwhelmed with the seriousness of my situation.

Between the actual arrest and my courtroom date, my landlord and friend, Anna, had made hundreds of phone calls attempting to find a way to keep me out of jail. She was one of those Christian types, and had told me many times about the Jesus she believed in and loved. I believed in heroin to make things right and it had worked for me so far. Recently, however, I had begun to question that. Nothing seemed to be going smoothly anymore.

Somewhere in the deepest recesses of my heart, I felt a small change. Something had penetrated that stone cold piece of rock that lay in the middle of my chest; a rock that was now beating irregularly due to the mix of heroin and cocaine I had shot into my vein minutes before entering the courtroom. I hoped this would be over and done with before it started to wear off.

After the last arrest, I had been told by the police that I wasn't allowed outside once the sun went down. Please! I hadn't been told what to do in many years, and certainly had never lived with a curfew, and I wasn't about to let it start now. For reasons I didn't understand at the time, it did put a small amount of fear in me, and made me begin to do some serious thinking about my life. It was the fear itself that made me think that I didn't have much to fear. I went out anyway, dodging police and hiding in alleys until I could get the drugs I needed to make it to the next morning.

My life was a mess and the time was coming soon when I wouldn't have a choice but to face up to it. Something had to happen; the life I was leading had no future in it and I couldn't stand the drudgery of it any longer. I had destroyed everything good that ever happened to me, and now I was destroying myself. I was thirty-two years old and literally hated the person I had become. How could anyone possibly like me when I couldn't stand myself?

My younger years had been rough ones. My dad served in the military in World War II and entered government service when he got out. To me, he personified the stereotype "buck sergeant" that young people dread when they enter the military. I resented his strict discipline at home, which included, "Yes, sir," and "No, sir," and felt as if I had to request permission for everything.

I admit I was the rebellious type, so that created a volatile chemistry between us. I realize now that things may have been different in my life had I yielded more to his discipline. But the fact is, I didn't. I believe that even at this point, God had His hand on my life.

I am in the middle between two brothers; Bob, the oldest, and Rik, who is younger. My younger sister, Laura, died of cancer in 1990 at the age of 29. My mom is a loving and compassionate person, and I know I've put her through major periods of grief.

Laura and I were very close, sharing the same bedroom. I remember waking up sometimes in the night, to discover that she was sleeping on my back. I never knew why, but it gave me a warm feeling of protection for her. Leaving Laura, and later losing her would greatly impact my life.

My parents took us many places. My dad was an avid skier so we all learned at an early age how to ski. When he was sent to Germany for three years, the family went with him. It was an educational experience. We got to see and be in places that a lot of people will never have the opportunity to experience.

When we returned to the United States, I had a very hard time adjusting. I am basically a shy person and I don't make friends easily. My relationship with my dad got pretty bad and I started thinking that I would be better off on my own. I wouldn't have anyone to tell me what to do and I could come and go as I pleased. That sounded pretty good to me, so I took flight and left home.

I hitch-hiked across the country a number of times doing whatever I had to do to survive. I never stayed in one place very long. I just kept moving. The police caught up with me from time to time and sent me home just so I could leave again. I was a wild child, to put it mildly, and continued that way for many years. I had no desire to change. I honestly believed I could live that way until I died, and I often hoped that day would be soon. Life had no meaning for me. Suicide attempts have left ugly scars on my arms, visible reminders to this day. I remember waking up in hospitals after I had overdosed feeling so angry to find myself alive that I went into uncontrollable rages. For some reason, I survived, but went back out on the streets to start the same things all over again. Talk about the dog returning to his own vomit! I had been given opportunities to straighten out my life but I chose not to. No, thank you. I didn't feel worthy.

I married at the age of eighteen, six months pregnant, but hoping somehow for a more settled life. I found out the hard way that pregnancy is not a good reason to get married; the marriage lasted only a year and a half. I gave birth to a beautiful little girl we named Candance (Candi). Her father got custody of her after three very short years. It was probably for the best anyway, but it didn't make me feel any better about myself.

Shortly thereafter, I met another man who was kind, compassionate, and very loving. I don't believe I was capable of love, although I thought I was. I had another beautiful baby girl named Melissa. Her father got custody of her when she was two. By now, that made me a two-time loser.

I got myself together for a very short period of time and held down a job at a local nursing home. A married man named Lance* lit up my eyes and made my heart smile. The relationship grew quickly and he left his wife to move in with me. Living together meant that I once again had someone to answer to and that caused the road to get somewhat rocky. For a month or so the love that this man showed me was enough to keep me from being numb on drugs all the time. When that rocky road got a few potholes in it, heroin once again became the love of my life. Lance began doing drugs too and we made a wonderful couple, fighting over who would get the last line of cocaine.

the name has been changed

We had a fight one day because we had no drugs and no money. The next time I saw him, he was hanging from a ceiling beam in the basement by some of the electrical cord he used for work. Once again I went on one of the frenzied heroin and cocaine missions that had brought me to the place I was today, sitting in a courtroom before the same judge who now knew me by name.

Would this self-destruction never end? I began to face the fact that I would be going to jail. What else could the judge do? There are only so many times that you'll get slapped on the hand and told not to do it again before they change your address for you. Oh, well, it would probably be about six months, and what's six more months added to the rest of the miserable life that I chose to lead?

Three men and two beautiful children were gone from my life, not to say anything about my family who no longer wanted much to do with me. What a pitiful excuse for a human being! What did I have to show for all those years except a heroin habit, a hardened heart, and a growing hatred for life in general?

Chapter 2
The Beginning of a Rainbow

A woman had entered the courtroom and was talking to Anna while all these thoughts were loosely and frantically skittering through my drugged mind. She looked like a nun to me; black skirt, white shirt and to this day, my imagination makes me think she also wore a habit. In any case, she seemed to represent that Jesus person Anna had told me about. What in the world was she doing here? Oh no, please don't tell me they want me to join a convent! The thought made me laugh aloud, not holding back, making everyone in the courtroom stare at me in amazement. The realization that I was now the center of attention made me laugh even harder. Anna and this woman whisked me out of the courtroom in a hurry, into the dreary hallway and on to a hard brown bench. Their faces were beet red and as I look back, I can understand why. Not only was I visibly and extremely high, I had acted like an idiot. I felt sorry for them and I might have been a little embarrassed too, but the thought of myself in a convent was just too much. I was on the verge of chuckling all over again when I realized that I had better get myself under control.

Anna explained that out of the many phone calls she had made on my behalf, there was one who had responded and her name was Gloria. After the introductions were made, Gloria told me that she had already talked with the judge about me, and she had a proposition for me to consider.

I was immediately suspicious. The powerful force of the heroin and cocaine was wearing off. Gloria told me about a Christian program in Virginia that she could get me into and that if I chose to enter, it would serve as the jail time that was so imminent. They left me to ponder the proposal, my mind going back and forth about it. I was really grateful that it wasn't a convent but wouldn't it be almost the same if I went into this Christian program? I had been in jail before and I could deal with that possibility. The thought didn't really scare me and I already knew a few people who were in the local jail now. I didn't know anybody in Virginia.

My thoughts went back into the courtroom where I had just reflected on my life, not being able to come up with one facet of my thirty-two years that was positive. My heart was discouraged, What's the use anyway? There wasn't much in this world I hadn't done or tried except this Jesus. What did I have to lose? Maybe I should give it a try; if nothing else, it would keep me out of jail for a while. Not only that, I would be on the road again and that's something that had always given me comfort. Hey, if I got down to Virginia and decided to change my mind, who would ever know? I knew that I needed a change; this gave me the opportunity to do just that. Even if it was just a change of location, it was indeed a change. Oh well, as Willie Nelson sings,

"On the road again, just can't wait to be on the road again."

Anna and Gloria looked at me with eager anticipation on their faces which made me smile. It seemed as if they already knew what my answer would be; they probably knew it before I did. I told Gloria that I would try it, although I made no promises as to what would happen and, for the moment, that was good enough for her. I couldn't think of too many things in my life that had turned out well. Why should it start now?

We went back into the courtroom with Anna and Gloria smiling from ear to ear and me thinking of my next dose of heroin. I hoped they would call my name soon; I was getting a little on the edgy side. After what seemed hours, my name was called. I stood up nervously while Gloria asked the judge if she could have a word with him. They spoke for a few minutes and the judge turned to me and asked me if I was agreeable to go into the program. Was this a joke, did he really think I would say no? Aw c'mon, just get me out of this courtroom!

"Yes, sir. I do."

"I order you, Linda, to complete one year in the Youth Challenge program in Newport News, Virginia. It will be arranged so that if you choose to leave before the year is up, I will be notified and you will be brought back to Massachusetts to serve your time in a different manner. Do you understand this?"

So much for my thoughts of reaching my destination and then leaving. I should have known!

"Yes, sir. I do."

"Good luck, Linda. Case dismissed."

Bang went the gavel. My life was about to change in many ways over the next few months, from the least expected to the most dreaded. But it would eventually mold me into the person I am today, a person I have searched for all my life. The colors of a rainbow had just started to form their hue, though still dull and smoky. I had a feeling that I was getting a choice for a new direction in my life. I could make the colors of that rainbow shine brightly so that the whole world would see, or I could blow it once again.

Although my body was starting to call out to me in need of heroin, something felt different. That distant, dull rainbow had appeared and given me a glimpse of what could be in the future. Just that one small glimpse made me wonder if there was a possibility that I could make that rainbow bright and colorful. It was a challenge, a slight ray of hope.

Over the next few weeks as I waited for all the arrangements to be made, I clung to that minute glimpse of a rainbow, unsure of what it meant. That rainbow, however, wasn't powerful or color-ful enough to make me stop heroin or cocaine. My last shot of heroin was done about ten minutes before I boarded the bus to Virginia. In my bag I carried two sets of clothes, two packs of cigarettes, a couple of ten mg. valium, and a few phenobarbital...to keep me from getting sick.

Haven't I heard somewhere that at the end of every rainbow is a pot of gold?

Chapter 3
I Saw the Light

I arrived in Virginia about sixteen hours later, a mental and physical wreck. The first part of my trip was beautiful. I nodded in and out of the real world, somewhat exhilarated by the feeling of the bus wheels beneath me. Another part of my life was inching away from me as I slowly left New England behind. The scenic colors of fall and the quiet of the few people on the bus made it quite peaceful and I took full advantage of the last high I would have in a long time. By now, I was determined that I was going to make this work. I had always been a strong-willed person and I knew that I could do it if I set my mind to it.

About the time we got to New York, however, I was beginning to doubt this whole idea, and especially myself. The boldness that heroin always seemed to give me was rapidly waning, and I considered getting off the bus at one of the many stops we made along the way. I took both of the valium I had, chewing them up and hoping they would dissolve and get into my system quickly, thus boosting my courage once again. I began to wonder what I had gotten myself into when the valium finally took effect.

In Philadelphia, a gentleman got on the bus and I have to say, he certainly was a friendly person. By now the bus was pretty crowded and he said, "Hi" to everyone as he walked down the aisle toward me. Wanting to be alone, I had taken the back seat next to the bathroom and he plopped himself next to me, grinning from ear to ear. Before long, I believed that he had gotten on that bus just to punish me.

It didn't take me long to figure out that he was flying on cocaine. No wonder he seemed so friendly! It was virtually impossible for him to close his mouth. From Philadelphia to Washington, D.C. was torture for me. The only time I got any peace was when he went into the bathroom to do some more coke. Then he would sit back down and move his mouth nonstop. It might have been the condition I was in, but half of what he said made absolutely no sense to me at all. When he got off the bus in Washington, I was so grateful that I wanted to get off and kiss the ground.

I still had about five hours left on the bus so I took a few phenobarbital, celebrating the end of my torture. That man made me wonder if I was that disgusting when I was high. Boy, I hoped not. I liked cocaine, but the high didn't last long and it seemed that once you got started on it you couldn't stop until you were ready to fall down. In my circle we called it chasing the dog. Heroin was my baby; it gave me a no-care attitude and it make me scratch a lot.

As I stepped off the bus, I was met by a lady named LeeAnn. (I have to change some names here, but its a nice Virginian name, don't you think?) She seemed like a really nice lady. I am especially shy and not at all talkative when I meet new people, so she did most of the talking. It was the basic, polite, southern welcome. How was your trip, how do you feel, etc... She let me smoke in the car but warned me that I had better enjoy it because once I got to the house it would not be allowed. Oh no, please don't tell me that! It had never even crossed my mind that I might have to quit smoking cigarettes too. My concentration had been on bigger and better things, such as heroin. I then proceeded to go one step beyond chain smoking; lighting a cigarette long before I was done with the other one. That slight glimpse of rainbow that

I had clung to for the last couple of weeks no longer had any color at all. I saw the sky filling up with clouds, getting black, and - was that a loud peal of thunder? A storm was brewing. I waited for the downpour of rain.

We got to the house and all I wanted to do was go to bed, but that was not what LeeAnn had planned. I sat in her office as she went through my things asking me questions that I strongly felt were none of her business. Who did she think she was? I thought this program was a Christian thing. Why was she asking such personal questions that I had no desire to answer? I was getting on the grouchy side and asked her to tell me why she had to know all these things. She said that it would help her to get to know me better so she would know how to help me. If she was really sincere about wanting to help me, she should just get out of my face and show me where I was going to sleep. I thought that my torture for the day had gotten off the bus in Washington, D.C. Did I really deserve this?

The normal routine was that everyone was up at 6 a.m., but LeeAnn said I would be allowed to sleep late because I had such a long trip. Thank you, thank you, a million times thank you. Now, can I please go to bed? She showed me my room and off she went. I got into my nightgown and dragged my weary body into bed. Fortunately, I don't remember too much about the next couple of days. What I do remember, I'd much rather forget.

I woke up at some point sweating profusely and freezing at the same time. It felt as if some destructive, foreign insect had attached itself to my stomach and was slowly ripping it apart, piece by piece. I had never prayed, although I had learned the Lord's Prayer when I was young, but during this time I prayed over and over again that I would die. I asked God to please take me; this was more than I could stand. Death seemed to be the best and only way out. I felt as if I was going to die, wishing with all my heart that it would be soon. As far as I was concerned, the sooner the better.

As with any addiction, this passed and I found myself grateful that God had not taken me too seriously and let me die. Then, for some reason that rainbow appeared again and it seemed the colors had gotten a little bit brighter.

I was getting into the routine of the program, not liking it much. I found out quickly that this program was not going to be an easy one. We were up at 6 a.m., no excuses, and had an exercise period for an hour. After breakfast we went to our rooms to get dressed and have time for devotions. I had a roommate named Cindy* who was a real nice person and she explained the routine of the program to me. I am grateful to her for she brought me out of myself. I think that if I had been left on my own, I would have just crawled into a shell and it would have taken people a long time to break down the walls and get to know me. We were expected to attend a daily Bible study and memorize scripture verses. We were tested on these things every Friday.

The women in this program shared in the cleaning, laundry and the cooking. We rotated these responsibilities weekly, and the cooking detail was especially difficult for me. I had never really learned how to cook, and cooking for fifteen people was a challenge even for those with experience. Afternoons were spent back in class, and the regimented schedule gave us very little free time until lights out at 10:00 p.m. We went to church at every opportunity, and everything pretty much revolved around Christ.

I had led the night life so long that frankly, it was really difficult for me to be awake during the day. The ten or so other women in the program all had problems of some form. Different problems, different situations, but all of us had become uncontrollable in various ways. Since most of this program revolved around the Bible, I was still pretty confused about how any of that could ap-

the names have been changed

ply to my life. I didn't understand it and no matter how hard I tried, I just couldn't grasp it. I don't think I'm a stupid person, but for some reason it was all beyond me. Cindy was a big help to me in that respect. All of the women were saying that they were born again. Once you were born, how could you possibly be born again?

I knew when I was coming off heroin that I wanted to die, but I didn't. Did that mean I was born again? This was the same thing that Anna kept telling me about, and it seemed to work for the people in this program. I was astonished that everybody seemed so happy in spite of terrible life experiences, and I began to pay more attention in the Bible classes and studies that we had.

I got along with most of the other women in the program. Cindy and I were good friends, and another girl named Pam* came to be a close friend. Pam was a nutritionist who worked in a hospital and had become addicted to drugs. Working in a hospital and knowing many doctors, she was able to get prescriptions for just about anything she wanted. Pam's family had a good deal of money, so they sent her from Texas to straighten her out.

There was Peggy,* who was exceptionally shy and didn't talk much. She was very private about how she ended up in the program, and although I remained friends with her for quite some time, I never really knew her. She is married now and has a beautiful little girl.

Joy* was an older lady who was an alcoholic. She had pretty much destroyed her family and almost herself. Joy didn't seem to get along with anybody. In my view, she had an attitude problem which could be viewed as "holier-than-thou."

Carol* was about 16 and a perpetual runaway with alcohol, drug, and men problems. Finally, there was "Willie Wonka." Willie had already graduated from the program but was still living in the house while working on the outside. Since coming off drugs I had somehow acquired an incredible sweet tooth and she would bring me goodies (mostly chocolate) after work. I always called her Willie - she was my chocolate factory.

There were other women in the program, but the ones I have mentioned are the most memorable. There was something strange to me. I could see changes in their lives and they were all saying that it was because they were born again. It kept coming up in conversation. This was beyond me, and I suspected that it could never happen to me.

This program had a men's home and a women's home in the same city and on October 12, 1986, we went over to the men's home to watch a movie. The movie was "The Cross and The Switchblade." It was about a preacher named David Wilkerson who went into the heart of New York city and talked with the gangs about Jesus. He broke down some really mean guys, and I related a lot of my life to the things that happened in the movie. Well, that proved it to me: this born again thing could happen to me.

What happened next is beyond any words and cannot be explained on paper, but it was the start of a new life for me. One of the men counselors, Mike, talked a bit about the movie. Then he started to read Psalm 116 which begins

"I love the Lord, for He heard my voice;
He heard my cry for mercy.
Because He turned His ear to me,
I will call on Him as long as I live."

Mike got to the second verse of that Psalm and a tear rolled down my cheek. I could not understand this; maybe I had something in my eye. I looked around hoping that nobody had seen my lone tear. I hadn't cried in years. I didn't think I was capable of crying. Mike continued to read the third and fourth verses which say:

*"The cords of death entangled me, the anguish of
the grave came upon me; I was overcome by
trouble and sorrow. Then I called on the name of
the Lord, 'O Lord, save me!'"*

I don't remember the exact moment that it happened, but I
found myself on my knees, not just crying, but sobbing. Gut-
wrenching sobs, tears now flooding down my cheeks, smearing
my makeup and soaking my shirt. My life had turned out to be a
pitiful, disgusting mess, and I had no one to blame but myself. My
soul was empty and my heart was black and cold. My sins were
overwhelming; sex, drugs, men, alcohol, stealing, and a lying, foul
mouth. I had hurt my family and friends over and over and all
they had ever done was try to love me. I had sold my body to get
the drugs that my body craved, a vicious circle. I had totally destroyed anything good that had ever happened to me in my entire
life. What had gone so wrong?

At that moment I realized that maybe God did love me and His
Son had died for me too, as unworthy as I was. The only words
that I was able to get out of my mouth as my body heaved with
sobs were the words that Mike had just read; "O Lord, save me!"

I asked Jesus to forgive all my sins, which were countless, and
I asked Him to come into my life. All of a sudden everybody was
hugging me, half of them crying and praising God. I was able to
accept those hugs with a new sense of what it meant to be hugged.
It seemed as if my body had been released from some unknown
power. I felt such peace and love, yet not really understanding
where it was coming from. I thought that maybe it was the Lord;
this must be what they called "born again." I felt high, but it was
so much better than any heroin I had ever done and this thought
made me feel guilty. I honestly felt like a new person. Could it
really be that I had changed? All those years on the streets being

carefree, doing drugs and whatever else I pleased had always made me feel happy. Could I really be happy without it?

Although I cried a lot for the next few months, I was truly happy. It seemed that my plumbing had somehow been broken. Every time I turned around, I was crying! I cried when we prayed, I cried in church, I cried when we sang songs about the Lord. I think the only time I didn't cry was when I was asleep, and I very well may have cried then too. I know now that it was a release for all the hurt and pain I had ever felt. Jesus had forgiven me and was giving me a chance to start anew, to find the person in myself that I had searched for all those years.

I thought of the miserable life I had been living. I hadn't been able to find lasting happiness, and certainly not love. Sure, I could continue to live from one heroin high to the next, but the valleys in between were getting deeper and deeper. Here was Someone who loved me first, as wretched as I was, and He was God! It was almost more than I could comprehend, but the Spirit of Truth bore into my soul. Jesus was the only One who could free me from the slavery of drugs. When He redeemed me, I found real freedom.

I had always felt that there was a piece of a puzzle that was missing in my life. I had tried to fill that puzzle with many things, but it still felt empty and hollow. I found that piece of puzzle on the night that I asked the Lord into my heart and my life. I had spent thirty-two years in a cold, damp, never-ending dark tunnel, but I was finally coming out. I had found the guidance that I needed. Life was worth living. Yes, I saw the light!

Chapter 4
A Temporary Blackout

I spent the next eight months learning all I could about Jesus Christ, who had saved me from my sins and made me a new creature. (II Corinthians 5:17) And a new creature I was! I never felt the need for drugs, or anything else for that matter, as long as I had Jesus. However, there was still so much I had to learn and the search for myself was not an easy one. There seemed to be many obstacles along the way; mountains to climb, valleys out of which to crawl. Now, the strong-headed nature that was Linda was a great advantage for me. It seemed that no matter how high the mountain or low the valley, if I turned to God, He would always see me through. My heart had been hurt so badly, it would take time to heal that injury.

God worked in ways that I didn't expect and although my patience often wore thin and I questioned my new belief, the profound happiness that I had found would have been truly hard to shake. The high that I got from the Lord was unbeatable and far outweighed any other high that I ever had. There was no drug that could compare, not even heroin.

The most amazing part of all this was that I didn't need to go out into the streets and sell myself or go down to the hock shop to sell some more of my turquoise rings I loved so much. This was a free high. Jesus Christ had paid the price for my sins when He died on the cross. How incredible to think that God could love me so much that He would send His one and only son to die for me, as nasty and unworthy as I am. This was my first glance at unconditional love, which would enable me to love and be loved - something that I had never really known. What a happy camper I was!

I lived every day for the Lord, striving in my own strength to become perfect in all that I did. The program gave me a good, solid foundation. Everything we did was to God, for God, and about God. Please don't get me wrong; I was still far from perfect just as I am today. The rebellious side of me crept up often. Truthfully, it still does, but not nearly as much as before I was saved. I had gone my own way for so many years; it was a mighty struggle for me to suppress my rebellion. I read about the many miracles that Jesus performed when He was on earth, and I knew that God had worked a powerful miracle in me. Just for me to feel true happiness was a miracle in itself. It was the kind of happiness that puts a perpetual smile on your face and gives you a warm feeling throughout your body, from head to toe. Nothing could ever top the joy that I felt in my heart and soul. It was the ultimate for me!

After I had been in the program about nine months, I got a cold that I couldn't get rid of. I was so sick that I had to go to the doctor. I had suffered many colds, as most of us do, but this was a cold that could beat all colds! My doctor put me on some antibiotics and told me to come back in ten days. This cold seemed to be immune to medicine. I went back to the doctor again and she prescribed a stronger medicine. By this time the cold had sapped me of my physical strength; it seemed as if I'd had it forever. I had been honest with my doctor about my drug addictions and other aspects of my life so she asked me if I would be willing to take the test for the HIV virus. At that point, I would have done anything to get rid of that cold.

While I waited for those results, I went on living my life, happy to be alive, knowing how much God loved me and would never let anything happen to me. I knew in my heart that I was extremely high risk and my chances of being HIV positive were very close to one hundred percent, but I just didn't want to think about it. I had finally found happiness after thirty-two years and I didn't want to think of anything that might destroy that happiness. My life had really just begun and I wanted nothing to destroy that.

I stayed on antibiotics during the two weeks I waited for the results of my test. By the time I heard from the doctor's office, my cold was gone. The new antibiotics must have done the job. I was home free! They scheduled an appointment for me.

At the doctor's office, I had to wait an unusually long time. Unknown to me, I was waiting for them to call a counselor. The doctor and the counselor were in the room when I walked in. I didn't need to have a load of bricks fall on me. I was smart enough to put two and two together and I figured out the results before they told me. Needless to say, I was HIV+ and it did put a bit of a damper on my new-found happiness and joy. Okay, a giant damper!

I dealt with it well at the time, talking sensibly, asking them how long I had to live. They told me four years and that would be four years at the most. (It has been nearly nine years now and I thank the Lord for every precious second of those years. I'd also like to say, "nah-nah-nah-nah-nah-nah," to those doctors, and if I could remember their names, I would be inclined to do just that. I know now that they had no way to predict the time I had left. This disease runs its course differently in everyone. No two cases are the same. I also believe they had no right to put a time limit on me. I had enough to deal with; I didn't need to count the minutes I had left.) I cried a lot, having finally learned how to cry. I had cried so much over the last nine months that I did not hesitate and wasn't embarrassed about it any longer. When I calmed down a little, they told me I could leave. What next? The one thing I was sure of was that I wanted nothing more to do with God.

I'm not the type of person who gets angry easily, but within the next two hours my anger rose to the boiling point. I can't ever remember feeling such a tremendous surge of anger and betrayal. What is wrong with this picture? God had taken me from a worthless life and had given me a reason to live. He had taught me how to love and be loved. He had shown me a person within myself that I never knew existed. If God loved me so stinking much, how could He let this happen? It is said that there is a fine line between love and hate, and as far as I was concerned, God had most definitely crossed that line. Once again, love had failed me. I had turned my life around, did a complete about-face, no drugs, no sex, no rock-and-roll, not to mention anything about cigarettes, and what do I get for it? I'm going to die in four years and that's four years at the most! For some reason this scenario just doesn't make any sense. Am I missing something?

I thought that life was bad on drugs. I guess I had learned it was unbearable without them. What in tarnation is going on here? Why live four years in misery and pain knowing that you'll die soon? I had lived in misery for thirty-two years and had finally found some happiness and had started to feel as if I might be worth something some day and what happens? Wham! Out comes the rug and I'm right back on the ground again. It had been hell for me that first week after so many years of heavy drug use. Coming off heroin was not a pleasant experience. I can remember many hours during that time that I had wanted to die, now I really wished I had died. What a hallucination that stupid rainbow had been. What a joke! No rainbow and forget that pot of gold!

In my anger and rebellion, I turned back to my original love - heroin. Oh, what bliss! Who cared if I was HIV+? I certainly didn't! I was careful with what I did. Just because I was going to die in four years didn't mean that I had to drag a lot of other people with me. At least I was going to die happy, even if it was self-injected happiness. God had done me wrong. I wanted nothing to do with any of that junk anymore. Cancel that plan! God proved to me that He couldn't be trusted. I could always trust heroin and, by golly, I had missed it too. How could I have been so stupid and so gullible as to believe that I could honestly be happy without heroin?

I never got back to the point of heavy addiction. I didn't have enough time. One day I stupidly stepped into the middle of an argument over drugs and my life came very close to an end, right then and there.

Once again, heroin had made me bold and I honestly believed I could stop the fight that had just begun. There I was, in the wrong place at the wrong time. An argument had started between two men; men I knew and considered my friends. Well, they were my "drug friends" anyway. The fight was over some money that had disappeared. As each man became more and more angry, I stepped between them thinking I could help calm things down. Wrong. Before I knew what was happening, the punches started flying. Not only did they not calm down, but I became the punching bag! I was knocked unconscious sometime after the second punch. I honestly don't remember, but it didn't stop there. One of the men was wearing steel-toed cowboy boots and he had apparently kicked me until he felt better. I think he presumed I was dead when he left and by all rights I should have been dead. The God that I had rejected must have sent a few angels to watch over me and I'm sure that the man who had inflicted the damage was shocked to learn later that I was still alive.

When I finally woke up, it was quite dark outside. Momentarily, I didn't know where I was and why I had decided to take a nap on the ground when I had a bed at home. Man, that heroin could sure make you do some strange things! I thought that maybe the dope I had used was a lot stronger than the dope I'd been getting, and somehow I had gotten where I was and had peacefully nodded off. Still confused, I lit a cigarette trying to get my bearings so I could get up and go home. I noticed a little blood on the tip of my cigarette, but I didn't think too much about it. I thought I had probably hit the ground and split my lip when I had nodded off to sleep. It suddenly dawned on me that it was a little chilly so I began looking around for my jacket. I didn't see one anywhere so I decided to get moving. I started walking, thinking that maybe I could warm up and figure out where I was at the same time.

I staggered along the road until I got to a main street and knew where I was. Thankfully, I wasn't too far from the hotel where I was staying so I decided to hitchhike home. As people passed me in their cars, they looked at me with absolute horror and I didn't understand why. These people in Virginia are a strange crew, I thought. Just what exactly was their problem, I wondered. I kept walking, hoping to get a ride but not really caring because I was close to home. God gave me two feet and those two feet had walked many a mile. Just keep moving, don't panic.

Up the road about half a block, I saw two police cars pulled up in opposite directions so that they could talk. They were probably having one of their coffee breaks, I thought. I began to plot the lie I was going to tell them to try to get a ride home. I meekly walked up to them and said, "Hi" and told them I had epilepsy and that I must have had a seizure. (I do have epilepsy.) I then asked them if I could please have a ride home. One of them looked at me and turned away gagging. Hey! I didn't think I was that ugly; this dude had a problem. I know I'm not beautiful, but as far back as I can remember, nobody had ever gagged at the sight of me. Had I changed in the last few hours into a repulsive creature? This was beginning to make me wonder if I had stepped into the twilight zone. Aw, c'mon, the dope wasn't that good! The other officer was a little green in the face but at least he wasn't gagging.

"Young lady," he said, "have you seen your face?"

Oh boy, talk about your question for the day! How did he ever get on the police force if he was that stupid? All I wanted to do was go home and I was hoping that one of these nice policemen would do his duty and oblige me by giving me a ride. I didn't know who was a bigger idiot, me for asking for a ride or him for asking me if I had seen my face. I was getting impatient and silently cursing myself for ever believing the police would help. Sarcastically, I said,

"No sir, it's pretty hard to look at your own face!"

"Well, you're going to the hospital," he said.

Now, didn't this just put the icing on the cake. I was thoroughly convinced that I was in the twilight zone.

The ambulance came and off we went, the medics cringing at the sight of me. Hi-ho, Hi-ho, it's off to the hospital I go! What is the commotion all about? Both of the cruisers had escorted us to the hospital, one in front and one in back. All the vehicles had their sirens blaring and I could see the red and blue lights going round and round. As we passed by the hotel where I was staying, I wished that they would just drop me off there. I had been a nurse's aide for many years and was perfectly capable of cleaning up a split lip. This was a fruitless expedition and would be another hospital bill that I wouldn't and couldn't pay. Oh well, maybe once I got to the hospital they would let me sleep.

Apparently, I had been in shock and could feel no pain, so I didn't realize how colorful and grotesquely swollen my face had become. There seemed to be a hundred people in the small cubicle of the emergency room where they wheeled me, all of them asking questions. So much for the sleep I had hoped for. As I began to watch the blood-soaked bandages piling up in a basin, I began to realize why so many people had looked at me in horror. Oh, that poor policeman who almost lost his dinner.

I came out of the twilight zone and began to remember what had happened. While being cleaned up I gave everyone the information they asked for and then the pain hit. I still hadn't been told the extent of my injuries, but once that pain hit there was no question in my mind that they were major. I asked for some pain medication and was told they couldn't give me any until after the surgery. Wait a cotton-pickin' minute here. What surgery? They brought a portable X-ray machine in while I went through the clean and question process.

I had a few broken bones they wanted to repair. I was then told that I had a few broken ribs. I had either swallowed or spit out the majority of my teeth, my eardrum had been damaged, my nose was broken (not the first time,) my jaw was broken in two places, the bone that held my eyeball in place had been broken, and my cheekbone had been shattered. Okay, that's quite an impressive list, but why do I need surgery, and what is this shattered cheekbone noise? My jaw had to be wired and since I no longer had any teeth, they were going to have to wire it to something. My cheekbone looked like a hard-boiled eggshell, cracked and ready to peel, but that surgery would have to wait until after my jaw was straightened out.

I'm sure that after being told this news my jaw would have dropped to the floor in amazement, but it was already just hanging from my face so the expression was not discernible. What a pitiful mess! Heroin, the love of my life, had turned on me once again and I was about to begin the process of having my face put back together because of that betrayal.

After about three weeks, my face was still quite colorful, but it was all together again, and they were getting ready to let me go home. The doctors kept me on a steady flow of morphine and they were gradually weaning me off it when I once again saw the light at the end of the dark tunnel.

I started thinking about some of the things that I had learned in my nine months of happiness and longed to have that joy back. I remembered reading the book of Job; he was such a godly man. I didn't have a fraction of that godliness, and look at what he'd been through. Everything he had, including his health, had been taken from him and he never lost his faith in God. God had allowed all of that to happen to him to test his faith and Job passed that test. He withstood all the pain and suffering, pulled through it, and died a blessed and happy man.

Although I didn't complete much formal schooling, I did get my GED later in my life. Now I had failed this test in a big way. Would I ever learn? God had shown me a new Linda. He had filled me with a love I never knew existed; a love which made me happier in those nine months than I had ever been in my life. I had turned God's love into hate, a hate of my own. I had rejected the best thing that ever happened to me. What was the matter with me? The temporary blackout was over.

Once again, a single tear rolled down my cheek and I knew that I wasn't going to throw away all that I had gained. I had become angry at God because I was told I was HIV+. I realized that I had inflicted that upon myself; it wasn't God's fault. Okay, maybe He allowed it, but it wasn't without reason. How could I be so angry at the One who loved me so much? My thoughts went back to the third and fourth verses of Psalm 116 and I quietly cried, thinking of the first time that I had heard them. It hurt my face terribly to cry but each tear that I shed reminded me of the lost life that God had restored. I was alive through Jesus Christ, who had died on the cross for me so that I could live.

Painfully, I kneeled by my hospital bed and asked for forgiveness. I didn't ask just once; I asked over and over again, filled with sorrow that I had almost ruined all that God had given me.

As I struggled and groaned to get up from the floor, that rainbow appeared again. It still looked beautiful, even though I was seeing it through severely swollen eyes. It was red and blue from end to end, sparkling with radiance. God had taken what some may call a death sentence and had given me life. I was unsure of exactly what that meant but I knew with all my heart, mind, and soul that God loved me and I loved Him. My life would someday be full and complete, and I would lack nothing, because He would be all I would need. The peace and joy that I once felt filled me again and I slept peacefully, free of all physical and spiritual pain.

My rainbow wasn't as colorful as my face at that point but the colors had become distinct, and how beautiful they were! It would take a lot of work, but with God's help, someday it would shine brightly enough for the world to see. There would be many tears but more laughter; failure that would turn into success, a once rocky road would become paved to help me reach that mountaintop. The pot of gold at the end of the rainbow was nowhere in sight, but I had begun to receive some of the riches that could be found there - the bountiful riches that are found in Jesus Christ, my Lord.

Chapter 5
A Long, Lonesome Highway

After I got out of the hospital, I stayed in a mission for a couple of weeks until I could get back in touch with the Youth Challenge program. I was hoping that they would allow me to rejoin. There was a Christian woman who ran the mission and we prayed and had Bible studies together. Because of my injuries, I was allowed to stay in the house instead of leaving every day from 8:00 a.m. to 5:00 p.m. I'm so thankful for that because the mission was right in the midst of the drug community and it might have been hard to stay away. Somebody once told me that when you became a Christian, life would be easier. I've learned there is much truth to that, but it doesn't happen over night. To be quite honest, being a Christian is the hardest thing I've every done in my life. It has also proven to be the most rewarding.

My two allotted weeks in the mission were almost up when the program called back. I was told that I would be welcome but that things would be a little different for me. I wasn't quite sure what that meant but I was so anxious to return that I didn't think too much about it. I suspected they would be a little more strict with me and that I would probably be given some extra Bible study and that was fine with me. The other women in the program knew I had gone back to heroin and this would give the staff an opportunity to make an example of me. I knew that everybody had undoubtedly heard about my being HIV+, but I had no clue that their reaction would be so negative.

I was about to get my first taste of the rejection which seems to go hand in hand with this virus. It's a rejection that too many people who are infected have to suffer. Many feel as if they are outcasts, not belonging anywhere in the world and having to deal with this disease alone. They have no one to help them when they are sick, no shoulder to cry on when they are sad or discouraged, and no church that will receive them with open, loving arms. For many, their families and friends have forgotten that they ever existed.

Everyone in the program seemed to be afraid of me. Even Pam, the girl with whom I had been the closest now wanted nothing to do with me. I was given my own dinnerware and it had to be washed separately, as were my clothes. One of the staff members was downright nasty to me and I began to question what the problem was. I had truly repented, but people just could not deal with my disease. In 1987 there wasn't a lot of education about AIDS, and fear and ignorance influenced attitudes. But weren't these people Christians? God's second greatest commandment was to love your neighbor as yourself and I don't remember any clause in there that says, "unless they have AIDS." This did not seem to be a consideration as far as I could see. They may have been afraid, but I was absolutely terrified! My life became like that of a leper while I was in the program. I had always been a loner and this gave me some more time to spend with God. The hugging and abundant love that all these people had once shown me were gone. I was lucky if anyone would pass next to me in the hall. I began to think of ways to leave without going on another downhill slide. I had learned that drugs were not the answer and the only people I knew outside the program used drugs. I knew that I would have to practice patience until God showed me a plan.

Since things weren't going too well in the program, I asked the pastor of the church we attended if I could speak with him. Naturally, he agreed and he seemed to understand my problem. Oh, this is great, I thought, at least one person understood. He cried when I cried, sharing his box of Kleenex. Hey now, here was compassion. We prayed together and I felt relief as I got up to leave. We had always hugged in the past, but when I went to hug him, he backed off. I was beginning to feel as if I should start yelling, "Unclean! Unclean!," as the lepers did in the Bible. He said that he would be praying for me but thought it best that I not mention my disease to anyone in the church. Suddenly I understood. I needed the unconditional love that I had once been shown by these people, and now things had really changed for me. I needed all these people now more than ever, and I was getting turned away left and right. The future was looking a little uncertain once again, but I thought about how my rainbow had been so breathtaking and beautiful that night in the hospital. No way, I would not let it dim this time. I may have been rejected by the program and the church, but God still loved me. I had God in my life and I didn't want to live without Him again; I knew that without a doubt. God had kept me alive for a reason and, although I still didn't understand why, I was determined to hang on.

Not too long after those experiences with rejection, I had to appear in court to testify against my attacker. Since I knew the guy who beat me up, and had identified the make and model of his truck, it wasn't hard for the police to find him. He was charged with attempted murder, but the charges were dropped to aggravated assault and battery with a dangerous weapon (his boot). I was terrified to testify against him, afraid that he would come after me. The police showed me some pictures they had taken the first night at the hospital and they were hideous. They didn't even look like the face that I saw in the mirror. What a terrible temper that man had! I hoped they would lock him up for awhile to keep him from doing that to anyone else. What incredible anger!

It horrified me to think that anyone could beat somebody as badly as he had beaten me with so little reason and leave them for dead as he had left me. It may have been my own stupidity to get into the middle of that mess, but how could he do that kind of damage to another human being? I thought back to how that officer had gagged and I couldn't blame him. I have a strong stomach, but I was very close to gagging myself when I saw those pictures.

The guy ended up with time served, about three months, and six months probation. He was asked to leave the state and never to return. Whether he did or not I do not know. I never saw him again. When my face gets too cold, the pin in my jaw freezes to remind me of the angels God sent to save me through one more ordeal.

It would have been easy to give in to anger and hatred for that man. I could certainly have wished a miserable, painful life for him. Satan was right there to encourage me and offer suggestions. But God's love would not allow that. His perfect love so consumed me that He brought me to the place where I could actually thank Him for allowing the attack to happen to me. Had I not been stopped in my tracks that night, I would not have landed flat on my back in that hospital bed, looking up, where God once again revealed His love and that rainbow. It may sound strange to say that I thank God for the beating that brought me close to death, but because of it, I found new life.

As Christians, we are to praise God for the good and the bad as difficult as that may be at times. For me, praising God for the rough times always seems to make things much easier.

Forgiveness wasn't quite as easy. God has taught me over the years that an unforgiving heart can literally destroy a person. It doesn't take long before unforgiveness can make one physically ill. But worse than that, God has specifically told us that if we regard iniquity in our hearts He will not hear us. Unforgiveness is sin, that's all there is to it. (Psalm 66:18) I look at it this way: If God forgave me as pitiful and unworthy as I am, who am I not to forgive others?

I stayed in touch with my friend, Anna, throughout all this mess. One day I made a collect call to her telling her of the long and lonesome highway I was traveling. In fifteen minutes the money for a bus ticket was waiting at Western Union for me. Anna is a great servant of God! I had come to know the God that she loved and believed in and I can never be thankful enough for her. Once again, she pulled me out of what could have been a major downfall. Dealing with my disease was hard enough, but I was having a more difficult time dealing with the way people were treating me because of it.

Anna had planted a seed and that seed had become a flower. In my mind I could see that flower standing tall until it was knocked flat in a windstorm. After a difficult struggle, it was restored to full bloom. Thinking of that flower, I could see a bright and color-ful rainbow on the horizon. The colors still appeared dull from time to time, blocked by clouds, but that rainbow would never lose its luster. It would become more vivid, adding brighter colors along the way.

The little wanderer was on the road again, heading back to Massachusetts. A different person would be returning; not the addict who had left a little over a year ago. I was a changed person and I liked the change. I had forgotten one thing though: all the good that God had created in me would not be seen by too many because I was HIV+.

The leper routine didn't stop in Virginia. I have no idea why I thought it might be different once I got home. It had slipped my mind that the majority of my friends were drug friends. Once you quit drugs, the friendships are no longer there. I was determined that I would not fall into that drug hole again. I became very close-mouthed about being HIV+. I had no friends because of my change in life-style. I had found a high that couldn't be bought, and as the vultures hovered above, waiting for me to lose that high, it made me see what I had left behind, and it wasn't much. It seemed that the few friends I did have who weren't involved with drugs slipped quietly away when they learned about the virus, as much as I tried to keep it to myself.

This virus has a way of separating those who really care about you and those who don't. At the time, I needed all the friends and support I could get. Losing this support was difficult to bear, but here again God met my needs. He taught me to lean on Him. He became everything to me: Father, Best Friend, Physician, Comforter. He was the Rock that never moved. God was always there for me no matter how badly people treated me. I could tell Him anything, laugh and cry with Him, and He never turned away. What a mighty God we serve!

I notified everyone I thought might also be at risk, hoping that they would get tested. This was a few hundred people, but it proved to be a fruitless task. They either didn't want to know or didn't care.

To this day, and it has now been nearly nine years, there are still people who are expecting me to go back to heroin. All I have to say is that it will be a mighty long wait! It truly was a miserable life. Why would I want to go back to that after finding such happiness?

Anna was helpful in so many ways. She helped me to work through the rejection that was so obvious. She went to a church in Andover but it seemed that at that time they were having a slight problem with the AIDS issue and, while they worked through it, I wouldn't be welcome. It was 1988 and AIDS was still a disease that wasn't talked about. Due to this silence, it was greatly feared and misunderstood. I understood that fear and to this day I still see too much of it. The majority of people who are still afraid either haven't been educated or don't want to be.

I went to another church for awhile but it just didn't feel as if I belonged there. Shy people find it difficult to make friends, and the people in this church didn't approach me. They seemed quite happy together and didn't have room for me. I was disappointed. I wanted a place where I could worship God in comfort.

I remembered that at the church I attended in Virginia, newcomers were always welcomed in a loving and special way. They were loved without being known and everyone tried to make them feel at home. Since I felt out of place, this church didn't work.

Anna introduced me to a couple who attended her church and who had a Bible study in their home. They were more than happy to have me join them, so once a week a friend of Anna's, named Jim, came to pick me up and a group of us studied the Bible together. This man eventually became an "adopted" father, a chauffeur, a shoulder to cry on, and one of my best friends to this day. He loved me for the person I had become even with the virus. He is a testimony to the many people who know and love him, including myself. I made my church with Anna and Jim during those months when I had no church per se, and that served the purpose well. They helped me to stay straight and grow in my relationship with God. They were my friends, and this was an important period in my life.

Anna and Jim told me a lot about a church in Andover called New England Bible Church and I knew in my heart that it was where I belonged. I had no idea that this church would be so instrumental in my life, my walk with God, and what would become my ministry. God blessed me with a special gift of fellowship, and that special gift is New England Bible Church. It's a place that I can call home.

Chapter 6
My Pot of Gold

New England Bible Church - there are no words to express what these four words mean to me. I consider it my church and the congregation is my family. They have been my support and have given me the love I need. They offer prayers on my behalf willingly and fervently. They accepted me when the rest of the world rejected me.

As in most churches, AIDS was not accepted with open arms. It was still in the "sinner's disease" stage, but God knew where He wanted me and opened the doors for that to happen. Pastor Chip Thompson is the shepherd of our flock and although I had only met him a few times, he had heard plenty about me from Anna and Jimmy. He arranged for a Christian doctor to come from Virginia to speak with the church body about AIDS in an attempt to help them understand it better. He was instrumental in the church's final decision. I am very thankful to him for that. The following Sunday night, I gave my testimony and my friend whisked me around the corner to a Dunkin' Donut shop while the members voted on whether they wanted people with AIDS to be allowed into the church. NEBC has been my home ever since.

I've heard many horror stories from people living with AIDS who have been rejected from churches and it breaks my heart. People with AIDS are human beings, and a lot of them are searching for love and comfort. In my opinion, a church should be the place to fill that need. I am so blessed that God sent me to a church where the people love the Lord above all else and are willing to do what God commands in spite of any fears they may have.

I have written a few things for some of the people who have become a big part of my life, and I think what I have written will give a clear picture of why God in His goodness placed them in my path. I pray the reader's indulgence as I publicly thank these dear friends.

The first one was written for Pastor Chip just because I love him. He is a "surfing" pastor and is really a unique person. The next one is self-explanatory, but before I share it I have to say, "I love you, Mrs. Joan!"

Pastor Chip

We all have a special friend,
He's in the hearts of all.
It makes no difference day or night,
He hears us when we call.

It may be sickness or sorrow,
Might be grief or pain,
It seems that every step we take
Is more a loss than gain.

God answers us with special gifts
To brighten up our day,
When life seems cloudy or so dark
That we can't find the way.

Our Mighty God and King of Kings
Sent His blessings from above.
My life is now worth living,
He has taught me how to love.

I love the Lord with all my heart
As all of us should do.

The special gift I'm thinking of
Is the gift I've found in you.

I got a special gift from God
And there's something I must do
I wrote this poem so I could say,
"THANKS FOR BEING YOU!"

MRS. JOAN - April 13, 1992

She is a radiant lady with flowing, blond hair. She is medium height and build, yet she seems to stand much taller in a very majestic way. When she is present, the room is filled with a calm peace that surrounds her, magnifying the love, warmth and understanding which fills her very being. She has three beautiful children who have been raised in love; in the way that God wants all mothers to do. It is evident in the people they have become, and in the way they stand apart from the rest. When she walks from room to room, it may appear that she's floating a little above the floor, somewhat as an angel might do, sharing the love and joy she has found in Him.

There seems to be a smile on her face at all times, and it perfectly fits the woman that she is. I am compelled to tell her I love her every time I see her. It is so important to me that she knows. She graciously looks the other way when I hand her husband his weekly ration of hard candy, saying softly and with great gentleness, "Nobody else better try to get away with that!" She understands and accepts me for the person that I am, rejoicing with me in good times and praying for me in bad times. It is a privilege and honor to know and be loved by her. God has blessed me with a special gift in this woman. Her name is Joan Thompson, the wife of Pastor Chip Thompson, the shepherd of the church I attend. Mrs. Joan, I love you!

This poem was written for my "adopted" Dad
HAPPY BIRTHDAY, JIMMY!

HAPPY BIRTHDAY, JIMMY

My own adopted Dad.
You've always been there for me
In good times and in bad.

You're a blessing to my ministry,
They call it "Driving Miss Daisy."
And I know there's been more than once
That I almost drove you crazy.

You are a good example
Of what a friend should be.
There are no words to tell you
How much you mean to me.

It seems that you are always there
To shower me with love.
And Jimmy, let me tell you,
I thank the Lord above.

And on this special day of yours
I'm blessed and honored and glad,
That God gave me a special gift-
My own adopted Dad!

I have written the last two poems for two dear women. My friend Carol is a very godly woman who has taken upon herself a ministry that has made my life much easier. Her ministry is to make sure I get rides to speaking engagements and to my doctor appointments. She makes certain that I get at least two hot meals a week, which church members supply. This ministry has been a real blessing. Living with AIDS and trying to manage my time, while being sick and tired of being sick and tired does not leave much energy for cooking.

Lisa (or Liser) is a close friend who also holds a special place in my heart. God has recently blessed her with the miracle of life, and I pray that God chooses to keep me on this earth long enough to see little John grow. These people are only a few of many, but it gives a good indication of the type of people who are members of NEBC.

A PRECIOUS GIFT

I know a special lady,
A real close friend of mine.
She's a precious gift that only comes
From God, the Great Divine.

A reflection of our Lord above
A bright and shining light
She's a bursting ray of sunshine
In the dark of night.

She's diligent in prayers for me
And I can feel it too,
She's always right there for me
When I am sad and blue.

It seems that happens often
When my body's racked with pain,
She always makes it clear to me
There's a crown that I must gain.

That crown that we all will wear
When we have run the race
And from what the Bible tells us
Heaven's a wonderful place!

When I finally win that crown
I know she'll wear one too
Right now and for the rest of time -
CAROL, I LOVE YOU!!

A BIRTHDAY POEM

Happy Birthday, Lisa
My sister and my friend
God gave to us a friendship
I know will never end.

And on this day that you were born
The Lord already knew
That someday we would be in Christ
And start our lives anew.

You are a special gift to me
You love and share and care,
No matter what my trouble is
You are always there.

You walk the walk and talk the talk
I'm sure that you don't see
The way that Christ shines through you
To people just like me.

He put you in my path of life
To often make me smile.
And I can't even count the times
You've walked that extra mile.

I praise God for your constant prayers
The way you show your love,
It's also for our friendship
That I praise the Lord above.

So on this special day of yours
I wish and hope and pray
That God will bless you always
In a very special way.

This poem to you comes from my heart
But now it's going to end
So HAPPY BIRTHDAY, LISA
MY SISTER, AND MY FRIEND!!

I have no gifts in public speaking, but many people at NEBC helped me to see that I could make a difference in the lives of many if I could talk about this disease and what brought me to the person I am today. Thus, God gave me a ministry. At first, I really struggled with it, and it had no name. It took about a year before God gave me what my ministry is now called, and that is LINDA. That stands for <u>L</u>ove <u>I</u>s <u>N</u>ever <u>D</u>ying <u>A</u>lone. There are too many people who are infected with this virus who end up living their remaining time left alone. Rejection seems to go hand-in-hand with AIDS. It is difficult enough to be sick twenty-four hours a day without having to do it alone. I have seen too many people die with nobody and I do not believe that God wants anybody to die alone. God is love, and His love is unconditional.

A perfect example of that unconditional love is New England Bible Church. I honestly do not know what I would do without this group of people who love me for who I am and pray for me and support me in all that I do. NEBC has made my rainbow absolutely brilliant with dazzling colors. A rainbow that could not get through the mist and haze for years now has a pot of gold. It is a gold in the form of loving and caring people, something that money cannot buy.

Chapter 7
Use Me, Lord

I always marvel at the things God has done in my life. He took what some might call a death sentence and gave me life. I am a whole person, a person I have grown to like, and one who still amazes me at times. The contrast is as broad as night and day; a totally different person. I spent the majority of my years hating myself and doing everything possible to destroy that miserable life. Now, I have learned how to love and how to be loved. Every pore of my being is now filled with a feeling that is so far removed from anything I have ever known. Love can come in many forms, and sometimes I think my heart will literally explode with happiness, just by knowing what love really is. I know that I have done nothing to deserve this, and I certainly do not feel worthy of it. Above all else, I know that God loves me no matter what.

I thought my rainbow was pretty much complete. I had even found my pot of gold. But God has shown me that I was wrong and He created many bright pigments I can't even name. These colors have an excellence of their own. They do not need names to give a ray of hope when darkness tries to set in.

Knowing God has so enhanced my life that I could never be thankful enough. Ecclesiastes 7:13-14 says,

> *"Consider what God has done; who can*
> *straighten what He has made crooked? When*
> *times are good, be happy; but when times are*
> *bad, consider: God has made the one as well as*

*the other, therefore, a man cannot discover
anything about the future."*

Living with AIDS has its ups and downs, but each day is a new day, leaving yesterday behind. It seems as though there is always something wrong with this body that has been so recklessly abused and is now paying the price. The apostle Paul had a thorn in his side and nobody really knows what that thorn was. My thorn is AIDS. As in the 12-Step programs, I take it a day at a time, not thinking about what tomorrow may bring. It helps that God always knows when I need a boost and then something happens that puts a smile on my face. Here are a few examples:

God has given my family back to me. It still hurts when I think of the pain that I put them through. My dad died before I had a chance to tell him that I loved him, after I finally knew what love meant. I was a confused and wild child, and my mom and dad put up with all the grief I threw at them. I love you, Dad. My little sister, Laura, died of cancer without my being able to see her one last time, but I know she is better off now, rejoicing around the throne of God. She died in June of 1990, and I saw my family for the first time in years in September of that same year. I talked with Laura on the phone not too long before she died, telling her I really wanted to see her. Her reply was, "Well, you better hurry." She knew that God was calling her home, and I never got to see her. She was the link that restored my relationship with my family, something that I thought was impossible.

Laura and I talked with each other several times before she died. I wasn't sure whether my mom knew about these conversations; but I learned later that Laura told her that she wished I could come see her once more. It was my mom who called to tell me about Laura's death, and that conversation opened the door for communication once again with my mother, and then with the rest of the family.

I now visit with them a couple of times a year, or as often as I am able. I always try to make it for Christmas. I have my mom, two brothers and their wives and four absolutely gorgeous nieces. What joy fills my heart! I can never undo the wrong I have done, but I am doing my best to be a daughter, sister and an aunt who is easy to love, someone who can make them feel proud. I thought for many years that I would never see my family again, but once again God swung those doors open wide. They know and fully understand about my having AIDS. Whether they realize it or not, they are a big support to me. Family is so important, and I am glad to be a part of them again.

Another sparkling and radiant color in my rainbow is a young man named Scott. Scott's mother was my best friend for many years. We lived together and shared our lives, including our children. This was how I became so close to Scott. Scott now stands taller than I am and weighs a few more pounds, but he's still that beautiful and loving child I knew as an infant. I sometimes think of him as the son I never had, and he's a very big part of my life today.

Scott started getting into trouble when he was about eight years old. Let me tell you, his mother paid for many broken windows because Scott and his little neighborhood buddy liked to throw rocks. Like myself, Scott was, and is, rebellious and didn't care much for discipline. I would baby-sit Scott and his brother while his mother worked, so I was often responsible for his discipline. Seeing myself in this young man has enabled me to understand him. Scott and I have always been able to talk and for quite some time I was the only one who could reason with him.

When he was nine, he was sent to live with his father, because his mother could no longer control him. Apparently the situation did not change in new surroundings. He began living on the streets and did not attend school. This eventually got him into a group home run by the state, where he is today. Scott has been hurt so much in his short life that he has a problem trusting people, which I understand. He has not had an easy life either, and my greatest hope for him is to see him happy and bursting with the same love that I have come to know. I know his potential; he is a fine young man. It has hurt him deeply to know that I have AIDS. We have spent many hours crying together as I assure him that I am going to heaven where I will have no more sickness or pain. I guess that isn't much consolation for a teenager who has finally found someone who really loves him.

I have been HIV+ since 1986, and have since graduated to AIDS, but Scott knows it is all in God's hands. He goes to church with me on Sundays, and we go home to have lunch and spend time together. Often I am sick and in pain, and I know that I get a wee bit grouchy with him, but he is understanding and wants to be with me even in those rough times. I would do anything for him. If it were not for this disease, I would attempt to get custody of him. I know that no judge would allow that at this point, and I really couldn't blame him. The thought is always on my mind, though. He means the world to me. So, Scott, my son, my son:

> *"When you read this, please know that I love you*
> *as if you were my own and don't ever forget it.*
> *God has angels watching over you; I know that*
> *for sure. Take hold of your life and run that race.*
> *You know it will never be easy, but you are a*
> *fighter, just like me. So, go for it, Dude!"*

God has given me the courage to speak about my life and this disease to many people. Many of the young adults write me letters afterwards that bring tears to my eyes and chills up and down my spine. Many times when I have been depressed and walking down the street trying to put the pain and sickness aside, someone will yell, "Hi, Linda!" and charge across the street to hug me. All of these things add to the palette of colors in the rainbow of my life.

Chapter 8
A Burst of Sunshine

God really does work miracles. He has performed many for me. God can take anything we think is impossible or totally out of the question and make it possible. (Luke 1:37)

When I gave birth to my daughter Melissa, I was still a wild and crazy person. I was finding it difficult to deal with my own life, and I knew I could never give her the life that she deserved. I gave custody of Melissa to her father knowing that she would be much better off with him. With all the mistakes I made in my life, this was something that I finally did right. A lot of people are still critical of me for that, but at the time I was trying to do what was best for her, knowing her life would not be good living with me. Christmas and her birthdays were always agony for me. I was so mad at myself for not being the mother that I should have been. While I was still doing drugs, the anger would pass quickly, as I would just numb myself out, escaping the pain.

Once my life was transformed by the precious healing of Jesus Christ, the pain of this separation ate at my heart in a new way. I knew deep inside that her father had given her a good life, and since I didn't want to disrupt that, I lived with the pain that I had brought on myself. Can you imagine walking into a teenager's life, telling her that you are her mother, then dropping the bomb that you have AIDS? I think not! I do my best not to hurt any-body, and I certainly would not hurt someone selfishly because of my own pain. A lot of prayer went into this situation. I prayed, my church family prayed, even people I do not know prayed. We all prayed the same thing - that if it was God's will, the day would come when I would see my daughter again.

Well, those prayers were answered. God unfolded the most intricate and incredible plan to make that happen.

It is a long, long story and involves many people, yet it went so smoothly, it still astounds me to this day. Eventually, I came to know Melissa's phone number and address. I even had pictures of her for a long time before I ever talked with her. For some reason beyond my understanding, I knew that I had to wait. As rebellious as I still can be, I know that God's timing is always perfect, but it seemed I would have to wait forever. Many times I had to sit on my hands to keep them from picking up the phone or I had to resist the temptation to drive by her house or school just to get a glimpse of her. But I did what I knew God wanted me to do, and now I am thankful for that. I thought the day would never come, but it did, when miraculously, her dad was bringing her over to visit me.

Yeehah! My wait was finally over! The first chance we had to spend time alone together was on Mother's Day, 1993, when I took her to a Mother-Daughter Tea at church. There is not a better gift anybody could have possibly given me than to be her mother once again, especially on Mother's Day. We talk on the phone at least once a week and see each other whenever we can. She doesn't live close, and since I am not allowed to drive, seeing each other is a little bit difficult.

Once, when I was talking to her about school, she told me about a girl who brought in a newspaper article which described me. My daughter told the girl, "Oh yeah, that's my mom." I want to tell you, I almost fell off the couch! After we hung up, I cried for hours, on my knees. She has grown into a lovely teenager and my prayer for her is that she will become a young woman of excellence, serving the same God who saved her mother.

Just when I think that God has made my life complete in every way, even with AIDS, He proves His love and blesses me with more. When I think I have it all, something else happens which makes me realize how truly blessed I am. Having my daughter back in my life is a very special blessing. She knows I have AIDS and accepts it. She holds no resentment towards me and understands why I did what I did. She could never have respected that Linda from long ago, but she knows me as the person I am now. Imagine that - more joy! My sweet Melissa - she's a burst of sunshine.

My other daughter, Candi, is still unknown to me. I want to see her again. It has been sixteen long, hard years, but since God worked it out for me to be reunited with Melissa, I trust that He will do the same one day with Candi. If it is His will, I know that someday it will happen. The wait was well worth it the first time; I am sure that it will be again.

Today, my rainbow sparkles with brilliance. I have found a pot of gold and a burst of sunshine. What more could I ask?

Chapter 9
An Upside-Down Rainbow

I met my friend Michael when we were working at the same grocery store. He was a real prankster and could always make me laugh no matter how the rest of my world appeared. He was the type of person who could overcome anything, and even during rough times, he always had a smile on his face. Michael is a person who touches your life from the moment you meet him and as time passes by, becomes a part of you.

The department I worked in consisted of a manager, an assistant manager, a full-time person and many part-time people. I was the one who worked full-time, so by company rules, I had to work one night a week. I always hoped that Michael would also work the same night. I went to work at 6:00 a.m. and worked until the store closed at 9:00 p.m. By the time the evening rolled around, I was ready for a few laughs, which Michael could always provide.

One evening, I was in the back room taking care of loose ends in an attempt to be out of the store at closing time. I was taking my handful of evening medications, when Michael walked into the room. He saw what was in my hand and casually asked what they were for. I named them off, but said that my AZT was Dilantin for seizures, and he just smiled and said, "Oh, okay." I hate to lie to anyone and Michael had grown on me, so the minute he walked out of the room, I felt very guilty.

I prayed a lot at work, for strength and patience (which I needed most of the time), and to praise God for keeping me healthy enough to work. I found myself praying for forgiveness for lying, and then finding peace again. The minute I said, "Amen!" I went out front and asked Michael if I could speak with him. We went in the back room, and as he stood there with that "Michael" grin on his face, I told him I was sorry that I had lied. I told him that I was infected with the HIV virus and was taking AZT. He replied, "I knew what it was, I take it too." I was so touched by the way he had respected my privacy that I just hugged him. We now had a bond that could not be broken, even in death.

We spent a lot of time together after that night. We went out for Chinese food or he would come down to my house in the evening. During my lunch hour, I would skip over to his house. He visited me in the hospital, and I would visit him.

I loved him so much that it took a heavy toll on me when he started to get really sick. It was so frustrating that there was nothing I could do for him. Well, that's not exactly true, I could pray. I prayed for him constantly, many times asking God to just take him to stop the suffering and pain. I was losing someone who had deeply touched my heart. I was closer to Michael in the short period of time that I knew him than I am to many people I have known for years.

Michael's family is absolutely incredible. They love each other deeply and are a very closely-knit family, something that is too rare in this world today. When Michael had been in the hospital for a while and there was not much more the medical community could do, his family brought him home.

While he was in the hospital, he changed the attitudes of many people and helped to straighten a very rugged and winding road that many other people with AIDS would have to walk.

Michael died December 31, 1991, having promised his sister he would not die the same year she was to be married (1992). I was spending Christmas at my friend Raeleen's home, and Michael's mom called me there to tell me that God had called him home. I was devastated. I had talked with him the night before and once again had prayed for God to take him. I felt guilty for that prayer. I said it because I could not stand to see someone I loved suffering so much for so long. Raeleen drove me home because I was a blubbering mess; I could not stop crying. Her children were young and could not understand why their auntie was so upset. That was the only time since I have come off drugs that I wished for a bag of heroin. I could not deal with the pain. A storm had brewed and erupted. But God, in His amazing grace, made sure that did not happen. This time God, and not heroin would help me deal with the deep, dark pain that taxed every inch of my body.

Michael was the first person with AIDS to whom I allowed myself to get close, and he was also the first to die. His was the first funeral I ever went to and the one that hurt the most. Now, I can no longer attend funerals; they are too painful, and there have been too many.

God and time have somewhat healed that wound, but I will never stop loving or missing Michael. I think of him often and still get teary when I'm reminded of him. I wrote Michael's parents a poem which I gave to his mom, and she has graciously given me permission to share it.

> *It's not for me to understand*
> *The way life works, what's in God's plan.*
> *But this I do know:*
>
> *Michael was a Special Friend,*
> *A gift from God above.*
> *He gave my life much happiness*
> *And a special kind of love.*

I'm really going to miss him
And all the things we shared.
His joy of life, his precious smile
Just knowing that he cared.

I praise God for his parents
And how they truly care.
They stuck by him through it all,
They were always there.

He filled a void in my life
That once was like a crater.
So instead of saying Good-bye,
I'll just say, "See you later!"

I never will forget him
He's always in my heart.
And when I see him in the sky
We never more shall part.

He had a special kind of life
That's really hard to beat.
Its such a joy for me to know
He's at our Savior's feet.

"The Lord giveth and the Lord taketh away.
Blessed be the name of the Lord."

Job 1:21b

Michael added a color to my rainbow that will never die or fade, a special color all its own. If you look at my rainbow upside-down, Michael's color would be the loop that's the longest, the one that looks like a gigantic smile. I thank God for that special smile. Although it may have been short-lived, it is a part of my rainbow for life.

Since Michael's death, I have remained friends with his family. They have been another blessing in my life. His sister, Pattie, recently had a baby girl, born on my birthday, and is now expecting another child. They are an exceptional family with hearts of gold, a love for God, and a deep love for one another. They share that love with all those who are fortunate enough to know them. I know that I will always have their support and love, so although God called Michael home, He left behind his family as a sparkling color in my rainbow.

Chapter 10
More About AIDS

People speak of AIDS as an epidemic. Any dictionary will define an epidemic as a contagious disease that spreads rapidly in a particular area. AIDS is no longer an epidemic. Today, AIDS can more accurately be described as "pandemic," because this disease is now geographically widespread over the entire world. It is not confined to the homosexual or drug communities, but is permeating the medical and heterosexual population as well. Testing blood of donors was not widespread until 1986.

In the short 15 years since the first AIDS cases were diagnosed, approximately 250,000 Americans have died and it is estimated that one million people in the United States may be HIV positive. The general public in this country can no longer ignore these deadly statistics. We can no longer pretend that it won't affect us or someone we love. We can no longer choose to ignore it and think about it tomorrow.

Americans must begin the battle against AIDS as we begin any battle. We must know the enemy.

AIDS is caused by the HIV virus (Human Immunodeficiency Virus). This virus destroys the body's immune system, leaving it vulnerable to many "opportunistic" infections. The body can no longer defend itself when the number of "T-Cells" (simply put: blood cells which fight infection) drops below 200 and a patient is said to have full-blown AIDS. A normal T-cell count is between 800 and 1500. Prevention is the only protection against this disease.

A simple blood test can determine if a person has the AIDS virus. Otherwise, there are symptoms which should not be ignored. For example, any swelling of the lymph glands (in the neck, armpits, or groin areas) which does not go away.

The virus may manifest itself in regular flu-like symptoms such as fever, aching muscles or joints, sore throat, headaches, diarrhea, "nightsweats," swollen glands or extreme fatigue. If you know yourself to be high-risk, and are experiencing any combination of these symptoms, AIDS may be a possibility.

The AIDS virus may attack a particular organ of the body: The bowels, (chronic diarrhea) the skin, (cancer) the lungs, with a form of pneumonia which causes shortness of breath and a nagging cough for no apparent reason.

AIDS does not affect any two people in the same way; it manifests itself differently in everyone. No one ever dies of AIDS. People die of many various illnesses and diseases which are intensified because they have no immune system with which to fight. The last time I had my T-cell count done, it was 206, so my immune system does not have much fight left. However, I am one of those people who does not take much stock in numbers. I know my body and I know how I feel. I know when I am sick, and I do not need anyone to take my blood to tell me. I have seen too many people learn they have a low count and shortly thereafter, they get sick. The mind can have a powerful impact on the rest of your body.

I had the "nightsweats" long before I was diagnosed, but just attributed it to my heavy drug use rather than thinking I might be HIV positive. I seemed to be tired a lot and had major nausea and swollen glands, but I learned quickly to live with these things and I continued to work. Now that I had found my rainbow, nothing was going to happen to take any of that luster and color away.

In February 1990, I was told I had cervical cancer. At that time, it was not considered an opportunistic infection. The Center for Disease Control did not put it into that category until 1993. I had been plagued with yeast infections for years and only by the grace of God did I learn to live with that.

I made an appointment with a local gynecologist to get a colposcopy. To make a long story short, this doctor did not want to deal with me because I was HIV+, although she wouldn't admit it. After three months, three appointments and three excuses, I finally asked if she had a problem with my disease. When she did not answer, I took that as a yes. I was out of there in a hurry, wishing she had been honest in the beginning. Three months can be a long time when you have cancer. Then I found a doctor in Boston who has become very special in my life. My memory often fails me, so I wrote a story about my hospital stay that I will share. I never finished my formal education in high school, but I did complete my GED later. While I was working on that, I realized that I enjoyed writing and wanted to pursue that interest. I took an English Composition course at a local college. Since I was on disability by that time, I was grateful that a local rehab paid my tuition and I paid for the books.

Writing has given me the opportunity to share my experiences and information about AIDS, but more important to me, however, is the opportunity to share my experiences with the God of the Universe. It is totally awesome to me that He wants to have a relationship with me, This story was originally written as an essay for that class. It is called "In God's Hands."

In God's Hands

I sat in the back seat of the car on that cold, raw
February morning. The clouds looked as if they
would burst, showering snow on all the commut-

ers who go through the drudgery of traveling back and forth to Boston every day. Sitting there, I pondered on what lay ahead of me. I had waited six long, agonizing months for this surgery. HIV can have its downfalls when it comes to treatment in the medical community. I had finally found a doctor in Boston to treat me who was caring, kind, and compassionate. Dr. Simon is a tall man with silver hair, which makes him look quite distinguished. I found a warmth in him, unlike any of the doctors I had dealt with before. He is a fine human being and an excellent doctor. We got to know each other very well.

When Jim, Kendalyn and I got to the hospital, we parked in the garage and went directly up to L-5 where my room would be. After we prayed, Jim and Kendalyn left, and the nurse came in to ask the usual hospital questions. She eventually left me to unpack and since I only planned to stay a week, I did not have much. I had brought my Bible and devotional books along with my Walkman and a hefty supply of tapes. Throughout my stay, these things became quite important to me.

I went into surgery the next day and although it was quite painful, Dr. Simon said he had removed all of the cancer with a total hysterectomy. It was two days later that my problems began. I was coming out of the bathroom and was halfway back to bed when I doubled over in pain. My stomach felt hot and bubbly, like a volcano ready to erupt. Tears rolled down my cheeks, and every pore in my body screamed with pain. I cried out and a nurse came running in. Things started happening fast; it was as if someone put time into fast-forward. The next thing I knew, Dr. Simon was at my side and it seemed like the room was filled with people dressed in white. Dr. Simon told me that my insides had become infected and that the infection would have to be removed. Tears sprouted from my eyes. I was terrified. I began praying as the mask was put on my face which put me to sleep.

When I woke up, it seemed as if I had tubes coming out of every orifice of my body. My days of heavy IV drug use had destroyed my veins, so they had to put the IV in my neck. The infection was so bad they left the wound opened and for the next two weeks, they continued to remove infection. I cannot even begin to describe the pain, but I felt every pick and scrape. The doctor told me that in all his years of practice, he had never seen an infection get so bad so quickly.

Thirty-three days after I entered the hospital, I was finally able to go home. I had lost a lot of weight, bones were sticking out all over and my cheeks were sunken. There are almost two weeks that I don't even remember, since my temperature was so high. The faithful prayers of my church and the astounding grace of God had sustained me through all that sickness and pain. Dr. Simon was wonderful, and to this day, I think of him as the grandfather that I never had, although he's not that old! Thanks and God Bless, Doc Simon!

Since then, I have had surgery many more times for various cancers and cysts. These cysts seem to pop up everywhere, and I must have them lanced or removed often because they never get better, only worse. When I went to Washington, DC, in 1992 to see the AIDS quilt and to visit my mom in Maryland, I developed a cyst behind my ear that needed to be lanced. I went to a clinic down there and the doctor who was going to lance it came into the room dressed like he was getting ready for a nuclear war. Universal precautions are good and should be used, but he honestly looked ridiculous! It took everything inside of me not to laugh. He looked so funny, as he changed his gloves four times during the process. He put four gloves on each hand! It was obvious to me that he had not dealt with too many people with AIDS. Whoever said suppressed laughter is the best kind was right. I laughed so hard my sides ached when he was done. Don't get me wrong, I understand the fear, but this doctor took it beyond fear. God bless him, though, for he treated me, and I am sure by the way he was dressed that he had overcome serious reservations about it.

I am so grateful for the many members of the medical community who have shown care and concern for me. My general doctor, Dr. Newsome, is a prominent member of that group of people. We have a good relationship, and he trusts me to know what is going on in my body. He is kind, gentle, and understanding and has been a real blessing to me. I went through six doctors who were deficient in the compassion and understanding categories before I found him. The medical field can still be cold and judgmental, and it is important for me to have people I can talk to, and who will talk with me, not at me.

I have neuropathy in my legs which has forced me to use a cane. I have lovingly dubbed that cane, "Cornelius," because it is my walking partner. At one point, my legs were so bad that it was suggested that I get a wheelchair. Well, I did get that wheelchair, but so far it is just taking up space in my closet! I have been getting acupuncture for quite some time, which has done wonders. My acupuncturist, Ted, is a real sweetheart and another person who prays for me and supports me.

The local VNA (Visiting Nurses's Association) has been right by my side for many years. They come to visit once a week and without them, I would be making many more visits to my doctor. I am so blessed to have them.

I have learned that people who work in operating rooms can be very accommodating if you request something. The last four or five times I have been put to sleep, I have asked them to sing "Amazing Grace." One time, a whole chorus of people got together for me, and it was so nice to go to sleep that way. When I had some skin cancer removed, the anesthesiologist agreed to sing, but warned me that he could not carry a tune. Well, I thought, how bad could it be? Later, I asked the Lord to put me to sleep quickly because that gentleman was not lying to me. His singing voice was the worst I have ever heard! God bless him though. I imagine it was a little embarrassing for him, and I was thankful that I went to sleep quickly!

When I weigh the pros and cons of the effects of the disease on my life, the former far outweighs the latter. I have learned to deal with whatever comes my way and still be a happy camper. This disease is a vicious circle, and all of us get what I refer to as the "Sick and tired of being sick and tired" syndrome. I praise God for the extra time that He has allowed me to live.

Hey. There's one thing about those dark clouds: They seem to intensify the deep beauty of a rainbow. As many people have already said, "I'm living with AIDS, not dying of AIDS!" The key word here is living.

Unfortunately, the diagnosis of HIV even when strongly suspected is not always easily confirmed because the blood test might not show "positive" for many months or years after exposure.

In the United States alone, it is estimated that by the end of 1995, 500,000 Americans will have been diagnosed with AIDS, and 320,000 - 385,000 will have died of AIDS-related complications. One in every 250 Americans are infected with the HIV virus. 80% of those infected do not know their HIV status. One American is infected with HIV every ten minutes! [1]

Internationally, AIDS will increase from an estimated four million in 1994 to 20 million by the year 2000.[2] Well over 90 percent of adults newly infected with HIV acquired their infection through heterosexual sex.[3]

It just makes good sense for people who know they are "high-risk" or suspect they have been exposed to have regular blood tests. It makes even more sense to be armed with information and protection. Ironically, some people are too casual about high-risk body fluids (blood and semen), while others get panicky about no-risk fluids (saliva, sweat, tears, urine.) When I speak to young people about AIDS, they ask if they can get AIDS through kissing. I tell them that it would take a gallon of spit for someone with AIDS to transmit the virus. A gallon of spit is a lot of saliva! Education is the answer.

The issue of AIDS is not going to go away. Chances are increasing that someone in your church already has AIDS. Churches, more specifically Christians need to address this issue today. Education, support groups, hospice care, love, all of these must come from the children of God to one another. Jesus said, "Love one another," and He promised to supply that love to those who are willing. Because of His tender mercy, God sent His Son to shine upon those who sit in darkness and the shadow of death. (Luke 1:78,9)

NOTES: 1. United States Centers for Disease Control and Prevention

2. AIDS in the World, Dr. Jonathan Mann et al,
   Global AIDS Policy Coalition, 1992

3. Global Programme on AIDS, World Health Organization

Chapter 11
Our Cross to Share

As Christians we have a responsibility to honor what God commands and to minister to the sick and needy by allowing them into our churches without judgment or prejudice. In Matthew 22:37 Jesus states,

> *"Love the Lord your God with all your heart and*
> *with all your soul and with all your mind. This is*
> *the first and greatest commandment, and the*
> *second is like it; Love your neighbor as yourself."*

There is no clause there that says, "unless they have AIDS." AIDS victims must be allowed into our churches. AIDS stands for Acquired Immunodeficiency Syndrome. It is a disease caused by the human immunodeficiency virus (HIV). The AIDS virus (HIV) may live in the human body for years and can be spread to others before any symptoms appear. It primarily renders your body unable to fight disease. AIDS cannot be cured. Scientists expect, if it is even possible, that finding a vaccine or cure will take many more years of research. The HIV virus is a slow acting virus and people may not show symptoms for ten years which accounts for the fact that the AIDS epidemic is mostly unseen.

As of February, 1992, the Center for Disease Control reports 213,641 cases of AIDS and 138,395 known deaths from AIDS in this country. The "known cases" they refer to are the ones that have been registered with the CDC. Those figures do not include the numbers of people who are living with the virus and have never been tested, nor does it include the rapidly increasing statistics which have occurred since those figures were made available. Many people don't consider themselves to be in the high-risk categories so they feel there is no reason to be tested. Remember, AIDS is no longer within the confines of the homosexual and drug communities. It does not discriminate and touches all walks of life.

Over the years, since the discovery of this virus in 1980, AIDS has been classified as a "sinner's disease." Some people feel that the people who have contracted the disease are "reaping the just punishment of their actions." Romans 6:23 says, "The wages of sin is death." There may be a good percentage of people with AIDS who are reaping what they have sown. But do we, as the body of Christ, consider the acts that may lead to cancer and heart disease as sins, and have we turned those people away from the church? Smoking is a major cause of cancer. Stress, overworking, and being overweight cause many heart attacks. If we are going to turn sinners away, we can't put classifications on the sin, for according to the Bible, they are all equal.

Aren't people with AIDS human too? Frequently, as Christians, we can get so wrapped up in the sin that we forget to look at the sinner. Christian's attitudes toward sin can affect their understanding of HIV. This misunderstanding can affect their desire to learn the facts and have a compassionate attitude toward those affected by AIDS. It sometimes happens that the disgust a Christian feels towards sin can turn into disgust for the sinner. It is easy for Christians to judge others but we must follow Christ who gave His life on the cross for us.

Now, isn't the way of the Christian the way of the cross? During an interview with Brother Tom, (Lazurus House, Lawrence, Massachusetts), I asked him why he felt that Christians were dealing negatively with the disease and he replied: "I think a lot of people don't understand the cross." Maybe that's too true for some to face. The AIDS crisis is a challenge to the people of God and an opportunity to show God's love in the way He commands in His word. It is demanded by God that the church of Christ follow the example of the Lord by being willing to take risks for the sake of others. Doesn't it say in Luke 9:23,24,

> *"If anyone would come after me, he must deny*
> *himself and take up his cross daily and follow me.*
> *For whoever wants to save his life will lose it, but*
> *whoever loses his life for me will save it."*

We need to touch those whom the world has rejected with love and understanding, and sometimes that means lending an ear or letting them know that you care. It's not a hard task; we do it everyday for friends and family. Too many people who are suffering with this infection have been rejected in many ways. Their friends and family seem to turn away and often they are shunned by their churches where they should find inevitable comfort. In the way that God has comforted us, we need to pass that comfort on to others.

> *"Praise be to the God and Father of compassion*
> *and the God of all comfort, who comforts us in*
> *our troubles so that we can comfort those with*
> *the comfort we ourselves have received from*
> *God."*

> *II Corinthians 1:4*

In the book, <u>AIDS: Ministry in the Midst of an Epidemic,</u> Hoffman and Grentz challenge Christians in this respect. They say, "The AIDS epidemic offers us a unique occasion to live as servants of God. It offers us a chance to respond with love to all the unfortunate people of our world. It gives us a way to show God's love, the nature of the Mighty One we worship. It is our calling as the people of God to reflect in our lives the image of our eternal God. At this time we have to rise to this challenge and be who God calls us to be: the people who serve others to the glory of God and for the sake of those who suffer." [4]

During the course of my research on the subject of AIDS, I interviewed two men of God to get their response to the AIDS issue. My pastor and friend, Chip Thompson, educated his congregation by having a Christian doctor who is active in the AIDS community speak with them and educate them. That church is now very supportive to those who are infected. Brother Tom, mentioned earlier, declared simply, that "...we must be at the service of God's will." They both agreed that it was "God's will" that they get involved. They also agreed that AIDS victims must be approached with the love of Christ. And Brother Tom reminded, "that the gospel of Jesus is unconditional love and compassion." Jesus Christ never turned anyone away. He was known to touch lepers, heal the sick, blind and lame, and give to the poor. Doesn't the Bible, which is the Word of God, command us to walk in the way that Christ did?

God has blessed me with a speaking ministry and I go to churches, schools and anywhere else where people will listen. I educate to the best of my ability and attempt to make people understand this disease and how devastating it can be to the victims, their friends, and families. I have seen AIDS victims die alone with no one to support them or be with them in their last moments. No human being should have to die that way and we, as Christians, can change that.

> *"Therefore, we do not lose heart. Though outwardly we are wasting away, yet inwardly we are being renewed day by day. For our light and momentary troubles are achieving for us an eternal glory that far outweighs them all. So we*

fix our eyes not on what is seen, but on what is unseen. For what is seen is temporary, but what is unseen is eternal."

II Corinthians 4:16-18

You see, my body is literally wasting away, but my eyes are fixed on God. I have AIDS and have been living with this disease for nearly nine years. It seems as if each year gets a little harder and I get a little sicker. I have God in my life, but what about all the people who are infected who don't have His comfort? Aren't we to be "fishers of men?"

I do understand the fear people have with regard to this disease. I've even heard some say that they don't want to look death in the face. The only way to conquer this fear is through education, not ignorance. As Pastor Chip said, "An issue ignored grows bigger and bigger." For every person who is living with AIDS, there are 100 who are diagnosed with the HIV virus. There are seven cases diagnosed a day in Massachusetts alone. The astronomical numbers given by the Center for Disease Control are something that we can no longer ignore.

I have personally written to fifty-five churches, ranging from Connecticut to Maine and of these fifty-five churches, only four have responded and two of those were to tell me thanks but no thanks. This is all on a volunteer basis; I ask for no money. God has called me to open the doors and hearts of people; to AIDS victims whether they are saved or not saved. I have no bitterness toward the negative response, that isn't what Christ would want me to do and I just don't have the energy to be bitter.

Through my speaking there have been good and bad results. The good far outweighs the bad, however. At one of the churches where I spoke, there was a gentleman who was also infected with AIDS, although the congregation wasn't aware of it at the time.

The pastor had been discipling him at home and wanted to open the doors for him with the congregation. The pastor called me to come to visit his church and I went joyfully and was well received. They had hours worth of questions and as they were educated, they became much less fearful and a lot more open-minded. When I finished speaking, the AIDS victim was introduced. I will never forget the scene as I was leaving the church. I turned around and he was surrounded by people who hugged him and wanted to get to know him better as a person, not just someone with AIDS. It brought tears to my eyes to see how he was surrounded by God's love through these people.

On a separate occasion, I had a pastor call me and arrange for me to come and speak with his church. We arranged the time and date and I was anxious to do it. He called me the week before I was to go. He was tongue-tied and obviously uncomfortable about what he had to say to me. Apparently, he had given a sermon on compassion and had included the AIDS issue. He told me that he had received so much negative response that he had to cancel. AIDS had not affected his church directly and the people felt that there was no need to deal with this issue. The two major concerns of the people were fear of my using the bathroom and drinking out of the water fountain. The lack of education there absolutely astounded me. He also told me that the youth pastor still wanted me to come and speak to the youth. How was that possible when the parents are so opposed to it?

Although I don't get paid for the majority of speaking that I do, God blesses me for it. I have stacks of letters from the teens I've spoken with that bring tears to my eyes. My joy is in knowing that they really listened to what I had to say and it made enough of an impact for them to want to take the time to write me. AIDS education is so important, and in order for those infected to be accepted for the people they are, everyone needs to be educated.

In addition to all the positive response I get, God has given me the strength and courage to keep going and I give Him all the glory. I am not a public speaker, I don't like crowds, and I'm a nervous person anyway. But God has put His hand on me and given me the courage to run the race that is His plan for my life. Since we have all made mistakes in life, we certainly don't have the right to judge another's actions and be unforgiving when God has so graciously forgiven us.

> *"There is only one lawgiver and judge, the one*
> *who is able to destroy. But you, who are you to*
> *judge your neighbor?"*

James 4:12

As Christians, we need to deal with the AIDS issue as Christ would have us do, not what we would do. We can show the love of God to those the world has rejected, the people who are touched by this deadly and devastating disease called AIDS.

It is said that we all have a cross to bear and as we know, the cross of Christ gives us an indescribable hope. AIDS is a cross that many bear. Let's make AIDS a cross that we can share with the many people who don't yet know the hope in Christ that we have already found. It can make such a difference in a person's life, turning night into day, as it has mine. We are the people of God. Let's accept the challenge and share the love of God that has so abundantly blessed our lives.

NOTES: 4. <u>AIDS: Ministry in the Midst of an Epidemic,</u>
         Wendell W. Hoffman and Stanley J. Grenz. Baker, 1990.

Chapter 12
Final Thoughts

There are literally hundreds of people who have supported me with love, prayers and anything else I could possibly want or need. I cannot even begin to name them all, but each one has contributed in some way to make my life the best it can be. I think they all know who they are, and I thank each one of them, deeply, from my heart. My life would not be the same without them. If I named each one and listed all they had done for me, this book would quickly turn into a boxed set. I love each and every one of you!

I guess in the last few years, I have gained some notoriety. Scott is always telling me that I am famous, but that is not what I want. I do not desire a name for myself. I give God all the glory for the person He has created me to be. He has given me the courage and strength to do things that I would never have done on my own. I know that without Him, I would not be alive to share my story with so many people. I hope and pray that I have touched a few hearts in my life and with this book.

As much as I am able, I spend most of my time speaking to high school students, churches, and other groups about AIDS, but mostly about what God has done in my life. I praise and thank God for every day He gives me, and for this opportunity to tell my story. I have often said that if I can touch one person, my job is done, and God is allowing me to touch many.

I also hope that I have given young minds enough education and honesty for them to know that AIDS is not something to take lightly. Our youth today will be our adults tomorrow, and it is important to me that their lives are the best they can be, and not shortened by this deadly disease that the world has come to know as AIDS.

This disease is not just sickness and pain. It is rejection, loss of independence, and painfully watching people you grow to love leave this earth. I cannot go to funerals anymore because they devastate me, and leave me unable to function for weeks thereafter. In many cases, it was AIDS that brought us together, but we had something in common, something that a lot of people in the world still don't understand after so many years.

No matter what your age, everybody needs to be educated about AIDS. I have heard many people say, "Why should I learn about that? It will never happen to me!" That may be true. But at some point, this disease will affect everybody in some way. It may not be you, but it could be someone you know and love. I understand the fear that people have, but if everyone were educated, it is possible that compassion and a better understanding might overcome that fear.

People with AIDS were "real" people long before they contracted the disease; people, just like you and me. God calls us to love one another, and that love is to be unconditional, no ifs, ands, or buts. The world might be a much nicer place to live if we could share the love in our hearts with others, no matter what. God has given me love in great abundance, more love than I thought I needed. I want to share that love with the world. I want my light to continue to shine brightly, and when God calls me home, I want people to remember the new person that God created in me. I do not fear death, God has promised me eternal life through His Son, Jesus Christ. When He calls me home, my joy will be complete with a rainbow that will never fade, an abundance of gold, and no more sickness or pain. To God be the glory!

My story is just one story out of the hundreds of thousands of people who are infected with this deadly virus. I am so blessed that God has given me a bright, sparkling rainbow and my pot of gold, but there are too many people who suffer with nothing. We have all sinned and fallen short of the glory of God, and I am sure that each of us has a few "skeletons in our closet" that only we ourselves and God know about. Christ never walked away from a leper, did He? God provides protection for those He loves, and it is important for everyone to know that when you meet a person with AIDS, you are more of a risk to them than they will ever be to you. With a suppressed immune system, any germ in the air can and will attack. Christ laid down His life for us and commands that we do the same. Isn't that reason enough to open your heart to those who are infected?

I urge everyone to educate himself or herself about this disease and share what you have learned with family and friends. Fear is natural, but I believe that education and God's love can overcome that fear. New England Bible Church is a good testimony to that fact. If God has filled your life with love, share that love. It might make a tremendous difference in the life of someone who has nowhere else to turn. In the process, you may learn a few things about yourself.

I must mention a few specific words of thanks on these pages. First and foremost, I thank God. He has given me life through AIDS and shown me a rainbow of hope that continues to grow brighter as the years pass. Thanks to the vast number of people who have become my support system and family, accepting and loving me for the person who was once lost, but now is found. Thanks also to Jan at Focus Publishing, who opened her heart and soul to what God would have her do. Finally, thanks to Anna, who introduced me to Christ, my Savior.

I pray that God uses this book to open eyes and hearts to educate those who still don't know the basics of this disease, even after so many years. I also pray that the people who read this, whether they are young or old, will take heed and not take chances as I did. I had a piece of the puzzle of my life missing for many years. That missing piece was Jesus Christ. I hope that anyone who feels they have that same emptiness will turn to God for the answer. His is the Way, the Truth, and the Life.

I have designated that all royalties from the sale of this book be donated to <u>Love and Action</u>, a national Christian ministry which serves people with AIDS. Volunteers assist the ministry, working through churches and communities to help with spiritual, financial and emotional support to those who have AIDS and their caregivers. It is a nonprofit, tax-exempt organization depending on the prayers and contributions of concerned individuals and churches. This organization is in the process of setting up a North American toll-free AIDS Hotline where youth may call for information from a Christian perspective. This is their address:

> Love & Action, Inc.
> 3 Church Circle
> Annapolis, Maryland 21401
> Tele: (410) 268-3442

As you read this book, you may be asking yourself how you can have the peace and joy I have found in fellowship with God. A heart in rebellion against God experiences no peace. The apostle Paul pointed out in Romans 5:1 that once we are justified by <u>faith</u>, we have peace with God through Jesus Christ, our Lord. If you have received Jesus as your Savior and the King of your life, that peace is yours. If you have not, you only need to believe and ask for forgiveness. Jesus is waiting at the door for you to invite Him in. It's as simple as that.

This book was written to and for the glory of God. He has given me so much and has made my life a life that is worth living. I am going to run that race and keep fighting because God promises me victory - a life everlasting with Him, with no more sickness or pain and where twenty-four hours a day, I can worship and praise the God who has created a new creature in me. And if heaven is anything like I imagine it to be, there will be rainbows everywhere!

Epilogue

Just about the time you think that God has blessed you far beyond anything you can imagine, He taps you on the shoulder with more.

One of the editors at Focus Publishing said that her prayer was that I would find my oldest daughter, Candi, before this book went to press. I had faith that this would happen before I died, but knew only that it would occur "in God's time." He knows the end from the beginning, and He knew the end of this story.

I have not seen Candi in 18 years. As I have said, she went with her father. He remarried, and Candi later went to live with a loving, adopted mother.

Recently Candi, now 21, was feeling blue. A yearning grew within her heart to learn what had become of her biological mother. She questioned her father who had no idea, but for some reason, though he lived in another state, he still had my mother's telephone number. It had been years since he had been in contact with my family. Indeed, it was not too long ago that I became part of their lives again.

One day, Candi dialed that telephone number and told my Mom who she was. Mom called me later and said, "You'd better sit down, I have something to tell you." Many people, near and far, had been praying about this, and now those prayers were answered. Since that day, I have talked to Candi, and we have exchanged photos in the mail. Grateful for that long awaited contact with Candi, I yearned to see her face to face.

I had an application from an agency in Boston called "For the Love of Life." "For the Love of Life" is an organization similar to the "Make a Wish Foundation," but it is for people living with AIDS.

I had always felt that any wish I could have made would have been frivolous. We all have wants and/or needs, but none of that seemed important enough to me. I had tucked the application away, suspecting that I would never use it. After I made contact with Candi, I started thinking that maybe this was the time to use my wish. I wrote Candi first to make sure that it was okay with her. She called me the day she got my letter, and with excitement in her voice invited me to, "Come on down!"

So I filled out the application stating that my wish was for a round-trip plane ticket to Georgia. I'll bet you're not too surprised to learn that I got my wish. There was only one other obstacle. I am on disability and don't have a lot of extra money. Candi has a small apartment and I didn't want to impose on her so I needed the money to stay in a motel the few days I was there. My pot of gold once again overflowed and some of my faithful brothers and sisters at New England Bible Church raised the money so that I could have a comfortable trip. I repeat, they are an incredible group of people and have done so much to make my life complete. Their love abounds.

The visit with my oldest daughter exceeded my highest expectations. There are no words in the dictionary that could properly describe it. I wasn't in my motel room for ten minutes when she called saying she wanted to come and take me out to dinner. Dinner turned into about four hours; the talk flowed easily and without reservation. We spent time together every day while I was there and before I had time to think about it, it was time to return home. We found that we had a lot in common, although we had spent too many years apart. She is excited to know that she has a half-sister (Melissa) and they now write to each other. Candi wanted to know her Mom and I wanted to find and know my daughter, so each of us found closure in our visit. I know that it won't end there. I hope that someday she can come up here to meet Melissa and all the people who are so much a part of my life. Once again, I must say, "With God all things are possible." (Luke 1:37)

On a sadder note, Scott is having a rough time. He ran from the program he was in, spent a while living in the streets in Boston, then ventured down to the village in New York City. I got a call from a TV talk show asking me to appear on the show to try to talk Scott into coming home. It worked and he came to stay with me until the state could find a program for him. The day before he could be put into a program he picked a fight with me and left. He had found freedom and didn't want to deal with the rules of a structured environment.

One evening I got a call from the police saying that he had been arrested for stealing, and would be held in a DYS facility until he went to court. In court, the judge told him that he had to stay wherever the state put him for a least six months or he would be put in a "secure" facility. Only time will tell what is going to happen, and only God knows. I will always love Scott, no matter what he does, but right now all I can do is pray. That TV show opened my eyes to the plight of many young people today. There are too many young people living in the streets who are filled with anger and hate. For them AIDS is not a deep concern, survival is. Scott used IV drugs while in New York and the majority of kids that he knew did too. What will become of these young people who will be our adults tomorrow? It truly breaks my heart.

God has chosen to make the circle of my life complete. There is nothing left in my life that is "undone." Whatever was broken is now fixed and on that day when God calls me home, and I can see

Him, I hope that He will be able to say, "Well done, good and faithful servant." That is my final wish.

Psalms 30:5 says that weeping lasts only for a night, but joy comes in the morning. My heart is full of joy and praise for a heavenly Father who has taught me how to love. Jesus was the only One who could free me from the slavery of drugs. He loved me first, as I was, a wretched sinner. Then He redeemed me and gave me true freedom.

Jesus said that he who does not love is not of the Father, for He is love.

"And they will know we are Christians by our love."